Carrie and Coco the Cat

Om KIDZ
An imprint of Om Books International

Om KIDZ | Om Books International

Reprinted in 2023

Corporate & Editorial Office
A-12, Sector 64, Noida 201 301
Uttar Pradesh, India
Phone: +91 120 477 4100
Email: editorial@ombooks.com
Website: www.ombooksinternational.com

Sales Office
107, Ansari Road, Darya Ganj
New Delhi 110 002, India
Phone: +91 11 4000 9000
Email: sales@ombooks.com
Website: www.ombooks.com

ISBN: 978-93-52760-22-0

Printed in India

10 9 8 7 6 5 4 3 2

Carrie and Coco the Cat

Paste your photograph here

My name is

____

Carrie is a **clever** little girl. She **can** tell the time on the **clock**.

Every morning, **Carrie** wears **clean clothes**. She always **combs** her hair **carefully**.

Coco

Carrie has a pet **cat**.

She is brown in **colour**.

Her name is **Coco**.

Coco

Coco, the **cat** is just as **clean** as **Carrie**. She licks her **coat** every day.

One day, **Carrie** is busy **counting coins** in her money box.

All of a sudden, **Coco** sees a mouse and runs to **catch** it.

Coco climbs over the **cupboard** in the bedroom.

She knocks over the
coffee cup in the kitchen.

Coco runs outside the house.

"**Coco**! **Coco**, stop!" **calls Carrie**.

But **Coco** is long gone.

Coco crosses the street and runs past the meadow. Some **cows** are eating grass there. “Mooooo…” they **call** out.

At home, **Carrie** is worried about **Coco**. The **clock** strikes seven. It is **cloudy** and **cold** outside.

Suddenly, **Carrie** hears a scratch at the door.

Carrie opens the door and finds **Coco** sitting there, shivering.

Carrie is very happy to see
that **Coco** has **come** back.

She **carries Coco** inside and **closes** the door.

Carrie cares a lot for **Coco**. She **covers Coco** in a blanket and holds her **close**.

Carrie feeds **Coco** some warm milk and her favourite **cookies.** **Coco** has had a long day. But she is happy to be in **Carrie's caring** arms.

Know your words

Naming words

Carrie	cat	cup
Coco	colour	cupboard
cows	coat	cookies
clock	coins	
clothes	coffee	

Describing words

clever	cloudy	cold
clean		

Doing words

combs	climbs	come
counting	crosses	closes
catch	call	covers

Sight words

can	close

Help Carrie find Coco.

Find the words from the word search.
Use the clue box given below.

B	W	F	C	C	I	J	W
B	B	W	C	L	C	N	V
C	N	S	O	E	O	R	O
F	A	B	I	V	W	C	B
D	N	B	N	E	D	H	K
R	B	X	S	R	R	I	F
C	A	T	W	K	J	D	D
E	C	L	O	S	E	B	V

CLOCK
CLOSE
COW
COINS
CAT
CLEVER

Match the following.

Coco •	• Call
Carrie •	• Coin
Cows •	• Clever
Count •	• Cat